THE RED INN
AND OTHERS

BY HONORE DE BALZAC

Copyright © 2017 by Astounding Stories

No part of this book may be reproduced in any written, electronic, recording, or photocopying without written permission of the publisher or author. The exception would be in the case of brief quotations embodied in the critical articles or reviews and pages where permission is specifically granted by the publisher or author.

Although every precaution has been taken to verify the accuracy of the information contained herein, the publisher assume no responsibility for any errors or omissions. No liability is assumed for damages that may result from the use of information contained within.

For permission requests, write to the publisher, put in subject "Attention: Permissions Coordinator,' at the address below, or contact us using our web site.

www.Astounding-Stories.com
Admin@Astounding-Stories.com

Whenever new book is published by Astounding Stories we will send you FREE eBook for your honest review.
www.astounding-stories.com/reviews
Join Our Email List NOW and get 5 FREE eBooks

All books in this Million Book Project by Astounding Stories are in Public Domain. They are published first time before 1923, or before 1963 and copyright was not renewed.

Proudly Created in the United States of America

TABLE OF CONTENTS

THE RED INN 5

THOUGHT AND ACT 10

A DOUBLE RETRIBUTION 40

ADDENDUM 55

DEDICATION

To Monsieur le Marquis de Custine.

THE RED INN

In I know not what year a Parisian banker, who had very extensive commercial relations with Germany, was entertaining at dinner one of those friends whom men of business often make in the markets of the world through correspondence; a man hitherto personally unknown to him. This friend, the head of a rather important house in Nuremburg, was a stout worthy German, a man of taste and erudition, above all a man of pipes, having a fine, broad, Nuremburgian face, with a square open forehead adorned by a few sparse locks of yellowish hair. He was the type of the sons of that pure and noble Germany, so fertile in honorable natures, whose peaceful manners and morals have never been lost, even after seven invasions.

This stranger laughed with simplicity, listened attentively, and drank remarkably well, seeming to like champagne as much perhaps as he liked his straw-colored Johannisburger. His name was Hermann, which is that of most Germans whom authors bring upon their scene. Like a man who does nothing frivolously, he was sitting squarely at the banker's table and eating with that Teutonic appetite so celebrated throughout Europe, saying, in fact, a conscientious farewell to the cookery of the great Careme.

To do honor to his guest the master of the house had invited a few intimate friends, capitalists or merchants, and several agreeable and pretty women, whose pleasant chatter and frank manners were in harmony with German cordiality. Really, if you could have seen, as I saw, this joyous gathering of persons who had drawn in their commercial claws, and were speculating only on the pleasures of life, you would have found no cause to hate usurious discounts, or to curse bankruptcies. Mankind can't always be doing evil. Even in the society of pirates one might find a few sweet hours during which we could fancy their sinister craft a pleasure-boat rocking on the deep.

"Before we part, Monsieur Hermann will, I trust, tell one more German story to terrify us?"

These words were said at dessert by a pale fair girl, who had read, no doubt, the tales of Hoffmann and the novels of Walter Scott. She was the only daughter of the banker, a charming young creature whose education was then being finished at the Gymnase, the plays of which she adored. At this moment the guests were in that happy state of laziness and silence which follows a delicious dinner, especially if we have presumed too far on our digestive powers. Leaning back in their chairs, their wrists lightly resting on the edge of the table, they were indolently playing with the gilded blades of their dessert-knives. When a dinner comes to this declining moment some guests will be seen to play with a pear seed; others roll crumbs of bread between their fingers and thumbs; lovers trace indistinct letters with fragments of fruit; misers count the stones on their plate and arrange them as a manager marshals his supernumeraries at the back of the stage. These are little gastronomic felicities which Brillat-Savarin, otherwise so complete an author, overlooked in his book. The footmen had disappeared. The dessert was like a squadron after a battle: all the dishes were disabled, pillaged, damaged; several were wandering around the table, in spite of the efforts of the mistress of the house to keep them in their places. Some of the persons present were gazing at pictures of Swiss scenery, symmetrically hung upon the gray-toned walls of the dining-room. Not a single guest was bored; in fact, I never yet knew a man who was sad during his digestion of a good dinner. We like at such moments to remain in quietude, a species of middle ground between the reverie of a thinker and the comfort of the ruminating animals; a condition which we may call the material melancholy of gastronomy.

So the guests now turned spontaneously to the excellent German, delighted to have a tale to listen to, even though it might prove of no interest. During this blessed interregnum the voice of a narrator is always delightful to our languid senses; it increases their negative happiness. I, a seeker after impressions, admired the faces about me, enlivened by smiles, beaming in the light of the wax candles, and somewhat flushed by our late good cheer; their diverse expressions producing piquant effects seen among the porcelain baskets, the fruits, the glasses, and the candelabra.

All of a sudden my imagination was caught by the aspect of a guest who sat directly in front of me. He was a man of medium height, rather fat and smiling, having the air and manner of a stock-broker, and apparently endowed with a very ordinary mind. Hitherto I had scarcely noticed him, but now his face, possibly darkened by a change in the lights, seemed to me to have altered its character; it had certainly grown ghastly; violet tones were spreading over it; you might have thought it the cadaverous head of a dying man. Motionless as the personages painted on a diorama, his stupefied eyes were fixed on the sparkling facets of a cut-glass stopper, but certainly without observing them; he seemed to be engulfed in some weird contemplation of the future or the past. When I had long examined that puzzling face I began to reflect about it. "Is he ill?" I said to myself. "Has he drunk too much wine? Is he ruined by a drop in the Funds? Is he thinking how to cheat his creditors?"

"Look!" I said to my neighbor, pointing out to her the face of the unknown man, "is that an embryo bankrupt?"

"Oh, no!" she answered, "he would be much gayer." Then, nodding her head gracefully, she added, "If that man ever ruins himself I'll tell it in Pekin! He possesses a million in real estate. That's a former purveyor to the imperial armies; a good sort of man, and rather original. He married a second time by way of speculation; but for all that he makes his wife extremely happy. He has a pretty daughter, whom he refused for many years to recognize; but the death of his son, unfortunately killed in a duel, has compelled him to take her home, for he could not otherwise have children. The poor girl has suddenly become one of the richest heiresses in Paris. The death of his son threw the poor man into an agony of grief, which sometimes reappears on the surface."

At that instant the purveyor raised his eyes and rested them upon me; that glance made me quiver, so full was it of gloomy thought. But suddenly his face grew lively; he picked up the cut-glass stopper and put it, with a mechanical movement, into a decanter full of water that was near his plate, and then he turned to Monsieur Hermann and smiled. After all, that man, now beatified by gastronomical enjoyments, hadn't probably two ideas in his brain, and was thinking of nothing. Consequently I felt rather ashamed of wasting my powers of divination "in anima vili,"—of a doltish financier.

While I was thus making, at a dead loss, these phrenological observations, the worthy German had lined his nose with a good pinch of snuff and was now beginning his tale. It would be difficult to reproduce it in his own language, with his frequent interruptions and wordy digressions. Therefore, I now write it down in my own way; leaving out the faults of the Nuremburger, and taking only what his tale may have had of interest and poesy with the coolness of writers who forget to put on the title pages of their books: "Translated from the German."

THOUGHT AND ACT

Toward the end of Venemiaire, year VII., a republican period which in the present day corresponds to October 20, 1799, two young men, leaving Bonn in the early morning, had reached by nightfall the environs of Andernach, a small town standing on the left bank of the Rhine a few leagues from Coblentz. At that time the French army, commanded by Augereau, was manoeuvring before the Austrians, who then occupied the right bank of the river. The headquarters of the Republican division was at Coblentz, and one of the demi-brigades belonging to Augereau's corps was stationed at Andernach.

The two travellers were Frenchmen. At sight of their uniforms, blue mixed with white and faced with red velvet, their sabres, and above all their hats covered with a green varnished-cloth and adorned with a tricolor plume, even the German peasants had recognized army surgeons, a body of men of science and merit liked, for the most part, not only in our own army but also in the countries invaded by our troops. At this period many sons of good families taken from their medical studies by the recent conscription law due to General Jourdan, had naturally preferred to continue their studies on the battle-field rather than be restricted to mere military duty, little in keeping with their early education and their peaceful destinies. Men of science, pacific yet useful, these young men did an actual good in the midst of so much misery, and formed a bond of sympathy with other men of science in the various countries through which the cruel civilization of the Republic passed.

The two young men were each provided with a pass and a commission as assistant-surgeon signed Coste and Bernadotte; and they were on their way to join the demi-brigade to which they were attached. Both belonged to moderately rich families in Beauvais, a town in which the gentle manners and loyalty of the provinces are transmitted as a species of birthright. Attracted to the theatre of war before the date at which they were required to begin their functions, they had travelled by diligence to Strasburg. Though maternal prudence had only allowed them a slender sum of money they thought themselves rich in possessing a few louis, an actual treasure in those days when assignats were reaching their lowest depreciation and gold was worth far more than silver. The two young surgeons, about twenty years of age at the most, yielded themselves up to the poesy of their situation with all the enthusiasm of youth. Between Strasburg and Bonn they had visited the Electorate and the banks of the Rhine as artists, philosophers, and observers. When a man's destiny is scientific he is, at their age, a being who is truly many-sided. Even in making love or in travelling, an assistant-surgeon should be gathering up the rudiments of his fortune or his coming fame.

The two young had therefore given themselves wholly to that deep admiration which must affect all educated men on seeing the banks of the Rhine and the scenery of Suabia between Mayenne and Cologne,—a strong, rich, vigorously varied nature, filled with feudal memories, ever fresh and verdant, yet retaining at all points the imprints of fire and sword. Louis XIV. and Turenne have cauterized that beautiful land. Here and there certain ruins bear witness to the pride or rather the foresight of the King of Versailles, who caused to be pulled down the ancient castles that once adorned this part of Germany. Looking at this marvellous country, covered with forests, where the picturesque charm of the middle ages abounds, though in ruins, we are able to conceive the German genius, its reverie, its mysticism.

The stay of the two friends at Bonn had the double purpose of science and pleasure. The grand hospital of the Gallo-Batavian army and of Augereau's division was established in the very palace of the Elector. These assistant-surgeons of recent date went there to see old comrades, to present their letters of recommendation to their medical chiefs, and to familiarize themselves with the first aspects of their profession. There, as elsewhere, they got rid of a few prejudices to which we cling so fondly in favor of the beauties of our native land. Surprised by the aspect of the columns of marble which adorn the Electoral Palace, they went about admiring the grandiose effects of German architecture, and finding everywhere new treasures both modern and antique.

From time to time the highways along which the two friends rode at leisure on their way to Andernach, led them over the crest of some granite hill that was higher than the rest. Thence, through a clearing of the forest or cleft in the rocky barrier, they caught sudden glimpses of the Rhine framed in stone or festooned with vigorous vegetation. The valleys, the forest paths, the trees exhaled that autumnal odor which induced to reverie; the wooded summits were beginning to gild and to take on the warm brown tones significant of age; the leaves were falling, but the skies were still azure and the dry roads lay like yellow lines along the landscape, just then illuminated by the oblique rays of the setting sun. At a mile and a half from Andernach the two friends walked their horses in silence, as if no war were devastating this beautiful land, while they followed a path made for the goats across the lofty walls of bluish granite between which foams the Rhine. Presently they descended by one of the declivities of the gorge, at the foot of which is placed the little town, seated coquettishly on the banks of the river and offering a convenient port to mariners.

"Germany is a beautiful country!" cried one of the two young men, who was named Prosper Magnan, at the moment when he caught sight of the painted houses of Andernach, pressed together like eggs in a basket, and separated only by trees, gardens, and flowers. Then he admired for a moment the pointed roofs with their projecting eaves, the wooden staircases, the galleries of a thousand peaceful dwellings, and the vessels swaying to the waves in the port.

[At the moment when Monsieur Hermann uttered the name of Prosper Magnan, my opposite neighbor seized the decanter, poured out a glass of water, and emptied it at a draught. This movement having attracted my attention, I thought I noticed a slight trembling of the hand and a moisture on the brow of the capitalist.

"What is that man's name?" I asked my neighbor.

"Taillefer," she replied.

"Do you feel ill?" I said to him, observing that this strange personage was turning pale.

"Not at all," he said with a polite gesture of thanks. "I am listening," he added, with a nod to the guests, who were all simultaneously looking at him.

"I have forgotten," said Monsieur Hermann, "the name of the other young man. But the confidences which Prosper Magnan subsequently made to me enabled me to know that his companion was dark, rather thin, and jovial. I will, if you please, call him Wilhelm, to give greater clearness to the tale I am about to tell you."

The worthy German resumed his narrative after having, without the smallest regard for romanticism and local color, baptized the young French surgeon with a Teutonic name.]

By the time the two young men reached Andernach the night was dark. Presuming that they would lose much time in looking for their chiefs and obtaining from them a military billet in a town already full of soldiers, they resolved to spend their last night of freedom at an inn standing some two or three hundred feet from Andernach, the rich color of which, embellished by the fires of the setting sun, they had greatly admired from the summit of the hill above the town. Painted entirely red, this inn produced a most piquant effect in the landscape, whether by detaching itself from the general background of the town, or by contrasting its scarlet sides with the verdure of the surrounding foliage, and the gray-blue tints of the water. This house owed its name, the Red Inn, to this external decoration, imposed upon it, no doubt from time immemorial by the caprice of its founder. A mercantile superstition, natural enough to the different possessors of the building, far-famed among the sailors of the Rhine, had made them scrupulous to preserve the title.

Hearing the sound of horses' hoofs, the master of the Red Inn came out upon the threshold of his door.

"By heavens! gentlemen," he cried, "a little later and you'd have had to sleep beneath the stars, like a good many more of your compatriots who are bivouacking on the other side of Andernach. Here every room is occupied. If you want to sleep in a good bed I have only my own room to offer you. As for your horses I can litter them down in a corner of the courtyard. The stable is full of people. Do these gentlemen come from France?" he added after a slight pause.

"From Bonn," cried Prosper, "and we have eaten nothing since morning."

"Oh! as to provisions," said the innkeeper, nodding his head, "people come to the Red Inn for their wedding feast from thirty miles round. You shall have a princely meal, a Rhine fish! More, I need not say."

After confiding their weary steeds to the care of the landlord, who vainly called to his hostler, the two young men entered the public room of the inn. Thick white clouds exhaled by a numerous company of smokers prevented them from at first recognizing the persons with whom they were thrown; but after sitting awhile near the table, with the patience practised by philosophical travellers who know the inutility of making a fuss, they distinguished through the vapors of tobacco the inevitable accessories of a German inn: the stove, the clock, the pots of beer, the long pipes, and here and there the eccentric physiognomies of Jews, or Germans, and the weather-beaten faces of mariners. The epaulets of several French officers were glittering through the mist, and the clank of spurs and sabres echoed incessantly from the brick floor. Some were playing cards, others argued, or held their tongues and ate, drank, or walked about. One stout little woman, wearing a black velvet cap, blue and silver stomacher, pincushion, bunch of keys, silver buckles, braided hair,—all distinctive signs of the mistress of a German inn a costume which has been so often depicted in colored prints that it is too common to describe here,—well, this wife of the innkeeper kept the two friends alternately patient and impatient with remarkable ability.

Little by little the noise decreased, the various travellers retired to their rooms, the clouds of smoke dispersed. When places were set for the two young men, and the classic carp of the Rhine appeared upon the table, eleven o'clock was striking and the room was empty. The silence of night enabled the young surgeons to hear vaguely the noise their horses made in eating their provender, and the murmur of the waters of the Rhine, together with those indefinable sounds which always enliven an inn when filled with persons preparing to go to bed. Doors and windows are opened and shut, voices murmur vague words, and a few interpellations echo along the passages.

At this moment of silence and tumult the two Frenchmen and their landlord, who was boasting of Andernach, his inn, his cookery, the Rhine wines, the Republican army, and his wife, were all three listening with a sort of interest to the hoarse cries of sailors in a boat which appeared to be coming to the wharf. The innkeeper, familiar no doubt with the guttural shouts of the boatmen, went out hastily, but presently returned conducting a short stout man, behind whom walked two sailors carrying a heavy valise and several packages. When these were deposited in the room, the short man took the valise and placed it beside him as he seated himself without ceremony at the same table as the surgeons.

"Go and sleep in your boat," he said to the boatmen, "as the inn is full. Considering all things, that is best."

"Monsieur," said the landlord to the new-comer, "these are all the provisions I have left," pointing to the supper served to the two Frenchmen; "I haven't so much as another crust of bread nor a bone."

"No sauer-kraut?"

"Not enough to put in my wife's thimble! As I had the honor to tell you just now, you can have no bed but the chair on which you are sitting, and no other chamber than this public room."

At these words the little man cast upon the landlord, the room, and the two Frenchmen a look in which caution and alarm were equally expressed.

["Here," said Monsieur Hermann, interrupting himself, "I ought to tell you that we have never known the real name nor the history of this man; his papers showed that he came from Aix-la-Chapelle; he called himself Wahlenfer and said that he owned a rather extensive pin manufactory in the suburbs of Neuwied. Like all the manufacturers of that region, he wore a surtout coat of common cloth, waistcoat and breeches of dark green velveteen, stout boots, and a broad leather belt. His face was round, his manners frank and cordial; but during the evening he seemed unable to disguise altogether some secret apprehension or, possibly, some anxious care. The innkeeper's opinion has always been that this German merchant was fleeing his country. Later I heard that his manufactory had been burned by one of those unfortunate chances so frequent in times of war. In spite of its anxious expression the man's face showed great kindliness. His features were handsome; and the whiteness of his stout throat was well set off by a black cravat, a fact which Wilhelm showed jestingly to Prosper."

Here Monsieur Taillefer drank another glass of water.]

Prosper courteously proposed that the merchant should share their supper, and Wahlenfer accepted the offer without ceremony, like a man who feels himself able to return a civility. He placed his valise on the floor and put his feet on it, took off his hat and gloves and removed a pair of pistols from his belt; the landlord having by this time set a knife and fork for him, the three guests began to satisfy their appetites in silence. The atmosphere of this room was hot and the flies were so numerous that Prosper requested the landlord to open the window looking toward the outer gate, so as to change the air. This window was barricaded by an iron bar, the two ends of which were inserted into holes made in the window casings. For greater security, two bolts were screwed to each shutter. Prosper accidentally noticed the manner in which the landlord managed these obstacles and opened the window.

As I am now speaking of localities, this is the place to describe to you the interior arrangements of the inn; for, on an accurate knowledge of the premises depends an understanding of my tale. The public room in which the three persons I have named to you were sitting, had two outer doors. One opened on the main road to Andernach, which skirts the Rhine. In front of the inn was a little wharf, to which the boat hired by the merchant for his journey was moored. The other door opened upon the courtyard of the inn. This courtyard was surrounded by very high walls and was full, for the time being, of cattle and horses, the stables being occupied by human beings. The great gate leading into this courtyard had been so carefully barricaded that to save time the landlord had brought the merchant and sailors into the public room through the door opening on the roadway. After having opened the window, as requested by Prosper Magnan, he closed this door, slipped the iron bars into their places and ran the bolts. The landlord's room, where the two young surgeons were to sleep, adjoined the public room, and was separated by a somewhat thin partition from the kitchen, where the landlord and his wife intended, probably, to pass the night. The servant-woman had left the premises to find a lodging in some crib or hayloft. It is therefore easy to see that the kitchen, the landlord's chamber, and the public room were, to some extent, isolated from the rest of the house. In the courtyard were two large dogs, whose deep-toned barking showed vigilant and easily roused guardians.

"What silence! and what a beautiful night!" said Wilhelm, looking at the sky through the window, as the landlord was fastening the door.

The lapping of the river against the wharf was the only sound to be heard.

"Messieurs," said the merchant, "permit me to offer you a few bottles of wine to wash down the carp. We'll ease the fatigues of the day by drinking. From your manner and the state of your clothes, I judge that you have made, like me, a good bit of a journey to-day."

The two friends accepted, and the landlord went out by a door through the kitchen to his cellar, situated, no doubt, under this portion of the building. When five venerable bottles which he presently brought back with him appeared on the table, the wife brought in the rest of the supper. She gave to the dishes and to the room generally the glance of a mistress, and then, sure of having attended to all the wants of the travellers, she returned to the kitchen.

The four men, for the landlord was invited to drink, did not hear her go to bed, but later, during the intervals of silence which came into their talk, certain strongly accentuated snores, made the more sonorous by the thin planks of the loft in which she had ensconced herself, made the guests laugh and also the husband. Towards midnight, when nothing remained on the table but biscuits, cheese, dried fruit, and good wine, the guests, chiefly the young Frenchmen, became communicative. The latter talked of their homes, their studies, and of the war. The conversation grew lively. Prosper Magnan brought a few tears to the merchant's eyes, when with the frankness and naivete of a good and tender nature, he talked of what his mother must be doing at that hour, while he was sitting drinking on the banks of the Rhine.

"I can see her," he said, "reading her prayers before she goes to bed. She won't forget me; she is certain to say to herself, 'My poor Prosper; I wonder where he is now!' If she has won a few sous from her neighbors—your mother, perhaps," he added, nudging Wilhelm's elbow—"she'll go and put them in the great red earthenware pot, where she is accumulating a sum sufficient to buy the thirty acres adjoining her little estate at Lescheville. Those thirty acres are worth at least sixty thousand francs. Such fine fields! Ah! if I had them I'd live all my days at Lescheville, without other ambition! How my father used to long for those thirty acres and the pretty brook which winds through the meadows! But he died without ever being able to buy them. Many's the time I've played there!"

"Monsieur Wahlenfer, haven't you also your 'hoc erat in votis'?" asked Wilhelm.

"Yes, monsieur, but it came to pass, and now—"

The good man was silent, and did not finish his sentence.

"As for me," said the landlord, whose face was rather flushed, "I bought a field last spring, which I had been wanting for ten years."

They talked thus like men whose tongues are loosened by wine, and they each took that friendly liking to the others of which we are never stingy on a journey; so that when the time came to separate for the night, Wilhelm offered his bed to the merchant.

"You can accept it without hesitation," he said, "for I can sleep with Prosper. It won't be the first, nor the last time either. You are our elder, and we ought to honor age!"

"Bah!" said the landlord, "my wife's bed has several mattresses; take one off and put it on the floor."

So saying, he went and shut the window, making all the noise that prudent operation demanded.

"I accept," said the merchant; "in fact I will admit," he added, lowering his voice and looking at the two Frenchmen, "that I desired it. My boatmen seem to me suspicious. I am not sorry to spend the night with two brave young men, two French soldiers, for, between ourselves, I have a hundred thousand francs in gold and diamonds in my valise."

The friendly caution with which this imprudent confidence was received by the two young men, seemed to reassure the German. The landlord assisted in taking off one of the mattresses, and when all was arranged for the best he bade them good-night and went off to bed.

The merchant and the surgeons laughed over the nature of their pillows. Prosper put his case of surgical instruments and that of Wilhelm under the end of his mattress to raise it and supply the place of a bolster, which was lacking. Wahlenfer, as a measure of precaution, put his valise under his pillow.

"We shall both sleep on our fortune," said Prosper, "you, on your gold; I, on my instruments. It remains to be seen whether my instruments will ever bring me the gold you have now acquired."

"You may hope so," said the merchant. "Work and honesty can do everything; have patience, however."

Wahlenfer and Wilhelm were soon asleep. Whether it was that his bed on the floor was hard, or that his great fatigue was a cause of sleeplessness, or that some fatal influence affected his soul, it is certain that Prosper Magnan continued awake. His thoughts unconsciously took an evil turn. His mind dwelt exclusively on the hundred thousand francs which lay beneath the merchant's pillow. To Prosper Magnan one hundred thousand francs was a vast and ready-made fortune. He began to employ it in a hundred different ways; he made castles in the air, such as we all make with eager delight during the moments preceding sleep, an hour when images rise in our minds confusedly, and often, in the silence of the night, thought acquires some magical power. He gratified his mother's wishes; he bought the thirty acres of meadow land; he married a young lady of Beauvais to whom his present want of fortune forbade him to aspire. With a hundred thousand francs he planned a lifetime of happiness; he saw himself prosperous, the father of a family, rich, respected in his province, and, possibly, mayor of Beauvais. His brain heated; he searched for means to turn his fictions to realities. He began with extraordinary ardor to plan a crime theoretically. While fancying the death of the merchant he saw distinctly the gold and the diamonds. His eyes were dazzled by them. His heart throbbed. Deliberation was, undoubtedly, already crime. Fascinated by that mass of gold he intoxicated himself morally by murderous arguments. He asked himself if that poor German had any need to live; he supposed the case of his never having existed. In short, he planned the crime in a manner to secure himself impunity. The other bank of the river was occupied by the Austrian army; below the windows lay a boat and boatman; he would cut the throat of that man, throw the body into the Rhine, and escape with the valise; gold would buy the boatman and he could reach the Austrians. He went so far as to calculate the professional ability he had reached in the use of instruments, so as to cut through his victim's throat without leaving him the chance for a single cry.

[Here Monsieur Taillefer wiped his forehead and drank a little water.]

Prosper rose slowly, making no noise. Certain of having waked no one, he dressed himself and went into the public room. There, with that fatal intelligence a man suddenly finds on some occasions within him, with that power of tact and will which is never lacking to prisoners or to criminals in whatever they undertake, he unscrewed the iron bars, slipped them from their places without the slightest noise, placed them against the wall, and opened the shutters, leaning heavily upon their hinges to keep them from creaking. The moon was shedding its pale pure light upon the scene, and he was thus enabled to faintly see into the room where Wilhelm and Wahlenfer were sleeping. There, he told me, he stood still for a moment. The throbbing of his heart was so strong, so deep, so sonorous, that he was terrified; he feared he could not act with coolness; his hands trembled; the soles of his feet seem planted on red-hot coal; but the execution of his plan was accompanied by such apparent good luck that he fancied he saw a species of predestination in this favor bestowed upon him by fate. He opened the window, returned to the bedroom, took his case of instruments, and selected the one most suitable to accomplish the crime.

"When I stood by the bed," he said to me, "I commended myself mechanically to God."

At the moment when he raised his arm collecting all his strength, he heard a voice as it were within him; he thought he saw a light. He flung the instrument on his own bed and fled into the next room, and stood before the window. There, he conceived the utmost horror of himself. Feeling his virtue weak, fearing still to succumb to the spell that was upon him he sprang out upon the road and walked along the bank of the Rhine, pacing up and down like a sentinel before the inn. Sometimes he went as far as Andernach in his hurried tramp; often his feet led him up the slope he had descended on his way to the inn; and sometimes he lost sight of the inn and the window he had left open behind him. His object, he said, was to weary himself and so find sleep.

But, as he walked beneath the cloudless skies, beholding the stars, affected perhaps by the purer air of night and the melancholy lapping of the water, he fell into a reverie which brought him back by degrees to sane moral thoughts. Reason at last dispersed completely his momentary frenzy. The teachings of his education, its religious precepts, but above all, so he told me, the remembrance of his simple life beneath the parental roof drove out his wicked thoughts. When he returned to the inn after a long meditation to which he abandoned himself on the bank of the Rhine, resting his elbow on a rock, he could, he said to me, not have slept, but have watched untempted beside millions of gold. At the moment when his virtue rose proudly and vigorously from the struggle, he knelt down, with a feeling of ecstasy and happiness, and thanked God. He felt happy, light-hearted, content, as on the day of his first communion, when he thought himself worthy of the angels because he had passed one day without sinning in thought, or word, or deed.

He returned to the inn and closed the window without fearing to make a noise, and went to bed at once. His moral and physical lassitude was certain to bring him sleep. In a very short time after laying his head on his mattress, he fell into that first fantastic somnolence which precedes the deepest sleep. The senses then grew numb, and life is abolished by degrees; thoughts are incomplete, and the last quivering of our consciousness seems like a sort of reverie. "How heavy the air is!" he thought; "I seem to be breathing a moist vapor." He explained this vaguely to himself by the difference which must exist between the atmosphere of the close room and the purer air by the river. But presently he heard a periodical noise, something like that made by drops of water falling from a robinet into a fountain. Obeying a feeling of panic terror he was about to rise and call the innkeeper and waken Wahlenfer and Wilhelm, but he suddenly remembered, alas! to his great misfortune, the tall wooden clock; he fancied the sound was that of the pendulum, and he fell asleep with that confused and indistinct perception.

["Do you want some water, Monsieur Taillefer?" said the master of the house, observing that the banker was mechanically pouring from an empty decanter.

Monsieur Hermann continued his narrative after the slight pause occasioned by this interruption.]

The next morning Prosper Magnan was awakened by a great noise. He seemed to hear piercing cries, and he felt that violent shuddering of the nerves which we suffer when on awaking we continue to feel a painful impression begun in sleep. A physiological fact then takes place within us, a start, to use the common expression, which has never been sufficiently observed, though it contains very curious phenomena for science. This terrible agony, produced, possibly, by the too sudden reunion of our two natures separated during sleep, is usually transient; but in the poor young surgeon's case it lasted, and even increased, causing him suddenly the most awful horror as he beheld a pool of blood between Wahlenfer's bed and his own mattress. The head of the unfortunate German lay on the ground; his body was still on the bed; all its blood had flowed out by the neck.

Seeing the eyes still open but fixed, seeing the blood which had stained his sheets and even his hands, recognizing his own surgical instrument beside him, Prosper Magnan fainted and fell into the pool of Wahlenfer's blood. "It was," he said to me, "the punishment of my thoughts." When he recovered consciousness he was in the public room, seated on a chair, surrounded by French soldiers, and in presence of a curious and observing crowd. He gazed stupidly at a Republican officer engaged in taking the testimony of several witnesses, and in writing down, no doubt, the "proces-verbal." He recognized the landlord, his wife, the two boatmen, and the servant of the Red Inn. The surgical instrument which the murderer had used—

[Here Monsieur Taillefer coughed, drew out his handkerchief to blow his nose, and wiped his forehead.

These perfectly natural motions were noticed by me only; the other guests sat with their eyes fixed on Monsieur Hermann, to whom they were listening with a sort of avidity. The purveyor leaned his elbow on the table, put his head into his right hand and gazed fixedly at Hermann. From that moment he showed no other sign of emotion or interest, but his face remained passive and ghastly, as it was when I first saw him playing with the stopper of the decanter.]

The surgical instrument which the murderer had used was on the table with the case containing the rest of the instruments, together with Prosper's purse and papers. The gaze of the assembled crowd turned alternately from these convicting articles to the young man, who seemed to be dying and whose half-extinguished eyes apparently saw nothing. A confused murmur which was heard without proved the presence of a crowd, drawn to the neighborhood of the inn by the news of the crime, and also perhaps by a desire to see the murderer. The step of the sentries placed beneath the windows of the public room and the rattle of their accoutrements could be heard above the talk of the populace; but the inn was closed and the courtyard was empty and silent.

Incapable of sustaining the glance of the officer who was gathering his testimony, Prosper Magnan suddenly felt his hand pressed by a man, and he raised his eyes to see who his protector could be in that crowd of enemies. He recognized by his uniform the surgeon-major of the demi-brigade then stationed at Andernach. The glance of that man was so piercing, so stern, that the poor young fellow shuddered, and suffered his head to fall on the back of his chair. A soldier put vinegar to his nostrils and he recovered consciousness. Nevertheless his haggard eyes were so devoid of life and intelligence that the surgeon said to the officer after feeling Prosper's pulse,—

"Captain, it is impossible to question the man at this moment."

"Very well! Take him away," replied the captain, interrupting the surgeon, and addressing a corporal who stood behind the prisoner. "You cursed coward!" he went on, speaking to Prosper in a low voice, "try at least to walk firmly before these German curs, and save the honor of the Republic."

This address seemed to wake up Prosper Magnan, who rose and made a few steps forward; but when the door was opened and he felt the fresh air and saw the crowd before him, he staggered and his knees gave way under him.

"This coward of a sawbones deserves a dozen deaths! Get on!" cried the two soldiers who had him in charge, lending him their arms to support him.

"There he is!—oh, the villain! the coward! Here he is! There he is!"

These cries seemed to be uttered by a single voice, the tumultuous voice of the crowd which followed him with insults and swelled at every step. During the passage from the inn to the prison, the noise made by the tramping of the crowd and the soldiers, the murmur of the various colloquies, the sight of the sky, the coolness of the air, the aspect of Andernach and the shimmering of the waters of the Rhine,—these impressions came to the soul of the young man vaguely, confusedly, torpidly, like all the sensations he had felt since his waking. There were moments, he said, when he thought he was no longer living.

I was then in prison. Enthusiastic, as we all are at twenty years of age, I wished to defend my country, and I commanded a company of free lances, which I had organized in the vicinity of Andernach. A few days before these events I had fallen plump, during the night, into a French detachment of eight hundred men. We were two hundred at the most. My scouts had sold me. I was thrown into the prison of Andernach, and they talked of shooting me, as a warning to intimidate others. The French talked also of reprisals. My father, however, obtained a reprieve for three days to give him time to see General Augereau, whom he knew, and ask for my pardon, which was granted. Thus it happened that I saw Prosper Magnan when he was brought to the prison. He inspired me with the profoundest pity. Though pale, distracted, and covered with blood, his whole countenance had a character of truth and innocence which struck me forcibly. To me his long fair hair and clear blue eyes seemed German. A true image of my hapless country. I felt he was a victim and not a murderer. At the moment when he passed beneath my window he chanced to cast about him the painful, melancholy smile of an insane man who suddenly recovers for a time a fleeting gleam of reason. That smile was assuredly not the smile of a murderer. When

I saw the jailer I questioned him about his new prisoner.

"He has not spoken since I put him in his cell," answered the man. "He is sitting down with his head in his hands and is either sleeping or reflecting about his crime. The French say he'll get his reckoning to-morrow morning and be shot in twenty-four hours."

That evening I stopped short under the window of the prison during the short time I was allowed to take exercise in the prison yard. We talked together, and he frankly related to me his strange affair, replying with evident truthfulness to my various questions. After that first conversation I no longer doubted his innocence; I asked, and obtained the favor of staying several hours with him. I saw him again at intervals, and the poor lad let me in without concealment to all his thoughts. He believed himself both innocent and guilty. Remembering the horrible temptation which he had had the strength to resist, he feared he might have done in sleep, in a fit of somnambulism, the crime he had dreamed of awake.

"But your companion?" I said to him.

"Oh!" he cried eagerly. "Wilhelm is incapable of—"

He did not even finish his sentence. At that warm defence, so full of youth and manly virtue, I pressed his hand.

"When he woke," continued Prosper, "he must have been terrified and lost his head; no doubt he fled."

"Without awaking you?" I said. "Then surely your defence is easy; Wahlenfer's valise cannot have been stolen."

Suddenly he burst into tears.

"Oh, yes!" he cried, "I am innocent! I have not killed a man! I remember my dreams. I was playing at base with my schoolmates. I couldn't have cut off the head of a man while I dreamed I was running."

Then, in spite of these gleams of hope, which gave him at times some calmness, he felt a remorse which crushed him. He had, beyond all question, raised his arm to kill that man. He judged himself; and he felt that his heart was not innocent after committing that crime in his mind.

"And yet, I *am* good!" he cried. "Oh, my poor mother! Perhaps at this moment she is cheerfully playing boston with the neighbors in her little tapestry salon. If she knew that I had raised my hand to murder a man—oh! she would die of it! And I *am* in prison, accused of committing that crime! If I have not killed a man, I have certainly killed my mother!"

Saying these words he wept no longer; he was seized by that short and rapid madness known to the men of Picardy; he sprang to the wall, and if I had not caught him, he would have dashed out his brains against it.

"Wait for your trial," I said. "You are innocent, you will certainly be acquitted; think of your mother."

"My mother!" he cried frantically, "she will hear of the accusation before she hears anything else,—it is always so in little towns; and the shock will kill her.

Besides, I am not innocent. Must I tell you the whole truth? I feel that I have lost the virginity of my conscience."

After that terrible avowal he sat down, crossed his arms on his breast, bowed his head upon it, gazing gloomily on the ground. At this instant the turnkey came to ask me to return to my room. Grieved to leave my companion at a moment when his discouragement was so deep, I pressed him in my arms with friendship, saying:—

"Have patience; all may yet go well. If the voice of an honest man can still your doubts, believe that I esteem you and trust you. Accept my friendship, and rest upon my heart, if you cannot find peace in your own."

The next morning a corporal's guard came to fetch the young surgeon at nine o'clock. Hearing the noise made by the soldiers, I stationed myself at my window. As the prisoner crossed the courtyard, he cast his eyes up to me. Never shall I forget that look, full of thoughts, presentiments, resignation, and I know not what sad, melancholy grace. It was, as it were, a silent but intelligible last will by which a man bequeathed his lost existence to his only friend. The night must have been very hard, very solitary for him; and yet, perhaps, the pallor of his face expressed a stoicism gathered from some new sense of self-respect. Perhaps he felt that his remorse had purified him, and believed that he had blotted out his fault by his anguish and his shame. He now walked with a firm step, and since the previous evening he had washed away the blood with which he was, involuntarily, stained.

"My hands must have dabbled in it while I slept, for I am always a restless sleeper," he had said to me in tones of horrible despair.

I learned that he was on his way to appear before the council of war. The division was to march on the following morning, and the commanding-officer did not wish to leave Andernach without inquiry into the crime on the spot where it had been committed. I remained in the utmost anxiety during the time the council lasted. At last, about mid-day, Prosper Magnan was brought back. I was then taking my usual walk; he saw me, and came and threw himself into my arms.

"Lost!" he said, "lost, without hope! Here, to all the world, I am a murderer." He raised his head proudly. "This injustice restores to me my innocence. My life would always have been wretched; my death leaves me without reproach. But is there a future?"

The whole eighteenth century was in that sudden question. He remained thoughtful.

"Tell me," I said to him, "how you answered. What did they ask you? Did you not relate the simple facts as you told them to me?"

He looked at me fixedly for a moment; then, after that awful pause, he answered with feverish excitement:—

"First they asked me, 'Did you leave the inn during the night?' I said, 'Yes.' 'How?' I answered, 'By the window.' 'Then you must have taken great precautions; the innkeeper heard no noise.' I was stupefied. The sailors said they saw me walking, first to Andernach, then to the forest. I made many trips, they said, no doubt to bury the gold and diamonds. The valise had not been found. My remorse still held me dumb. When I wanted to speak, a pitiless voice cried out to me, *'You meant to commit that crime!'* All was against me, even myself. They asked me about my comrade, and I completely exonerated him. Then they said to me: 'The crime must lie between you, your comrade, the innkeeper, and his wife. This morning all the windows and doors were found securely fastened.' At those words," continued the poor fellow, "I had neither voice, nor strength, nor soul to answer. More sure of my comrade than I could be of myself, I could not accuse him. I saw that we were both thought equally guilty of the murder, and that I was considered the most clumsy. I tried to explain the crime by somnambulism, and so protect my friend; but there I rambled and contradicted myself. No, I am lost. I read my condemnation in the eyes of my judges. They smiled incredulously. All is over. No more uncertainty. To-morrow I shall be shot. I am not thinking of myself," he went on after a pause, "but of my poor mother." Then he stopped, looked up to heaven, and shed no tears; his eyes were dry and strongly convulsed. "Frederic—"

["Ah! true," cried Monsieur Hermann, with an air of triumph. "Yes, the other's name was Frederic, Frederic! I remember now!"

My neighbor touched my foot, and made me a sign to look at Monsieur Taillefer. The former purveyor had negligently dropped his hand over his eyes, but between the interstices of his fingers we thought we caught a darkling flame proceeding from them.

"Hein?" she said in my ear, "what if his name were Frederic?"

I answered with a glance, which said to her: "Silence!"

Hermann continued:]

"Frederic!" cried the young surgeon, "Frederic basely deserted me. He must have been afraid. Perhaps he is still hidden in the inn, for our horses were both in the courtyard this morning. What an incomprehensible mystery!" he went on, after a moment's silence. "Somnambulism! somnambulism? I never had but one attack in my life, and that was when I was six years old. Must I go from this earth," he cried, striking the ground with his foot, "carrying with me all there is of friendship in the world? Shall I die a double death, doubting a fraternal love begun when we were only five years old, and continued through school and college? Where is Frederic?"

He wept. Can it be that we cling more to a sentiment than to life?

"Let us go in," he said; "I prefer to be in my cell. I do not wish to be seen weeping. I shall go courageously to death, but I cannot play the heroic at all moments; I own I regret my beautiful young life. All last night I could not sleep; I remembered the scenes of my childhood; I fancied I was running in the fields. Ah! I had a future," he said, suddenly interrupting himself; "and now, twelve men, a sub-lieutenant shouting 'Carry-arms, aim, fire!' a roll of drums, and infamy!

that's my future now. Oh! there must be a God, or it would all be too senseless."

Then he took me in his arms and pressed me to him with all his strength.

"You are the last man, the last friend to whom I can show my soul. You will be set at liberty, you will see your mother! I don't know whether you are rich or poor, but no matter! you are all the world to me. They won't fight always, 'ceux-ci.' Well, when there's peace, will you go to Beauvais? If my mother has survived the fatal news of my death, you will find her there. Say to her the comforting words, 'He was innocent!' She will believe you. I am going to write to her; but you must take her my last look; you must tell her that you were the last man whose hand I pressed. Oh, she'll love you, the poor woman! you, my last friend. Here," he said, after a moment's silence, during which he was overcome by the weight of his recollections, "all, officers and soldiers, are unknown to me; I am an object of horror to them. If it were not for you my innocence would be a secret between God and myself."

I swore to sacredly fulfil his last wishes. My words, the emotion I showed touched him. Soon after that the soldiers came to take him again before the council of war. He was condemned to death. I am ignorant of the formalities that followed or accompanied this judgment, nor do I know whether the young surgeon defended his life or not; but he expected to be executed on the following day, and he spent the night in writing to his mother.

"We shall both be free to-day," he said, smiling, when I went to see him the next morning. "I am told that the general has signed your pardon."

I was silent, and looked at him closely so as to carve his features, as it were, on my memory. Presently an expression of disgust crossed his face.

"I have been very cowardly," he said. "During all last night I begged for mercy of these walls," and he pointed to the sides of his dungeon. "Yes, yes, I howled with despair, I rebelled, I suffered the most awful moral agony—I was alone! Now I think of what others will say of me. Courage is a garment to put on. I desire to go decently to death, therefore—"

A DOUBLE RETRIBUTION

"Oh, stop! stop!" cried the young lady who had asked for this history, interrupting the narrator suddenly. "Say no more; let me remain in uncertainty and believe that he was saved. If I hear now that he was shot I shall not sleep all night. To-morrow you shall tell me the rest."

We rose from table. My neighbor in accepting Monsieur Hermann's arm, said to him—

"I suppose he was shot, was he not?"

"Yes. I was present at the execution."

"Oh! monsieur," she said, "how could you—"

"He desired it, madame. There was something really dreadful in following the funeral of a living man, a man my heart cared for, an innocent man! The poor young fellow never ceased to look at me. He seemed to live only in me. He wanted, he said, that I should carry to his mother his last sigh."

"And did you?"

"At the peace of Amiens I went to France, for the purpose of taking to the mother those blessed words, 'He was innocent.' I religiously undertook that pilgrimage. But Madame Magnan had died of consumption. It was not without deep emotion that I burned the letter of which I was the bearer. You will perhaps smile at my German imagination, but I see a drama of sad sublimity in the eternal secrecy which engulfed those parting words cast between two graves, unknown to all creation, like the cry uttered in a desert by some lonely traveller whom a lion seizes."

"And if," I said, interrupting him, "you were brought face to face with a man now in this room, and were told, 'This is the murderer!' would not that be another drama? And what would you do?"

Monsieur Hermann looked for his hat and went away.

"You are behaving like a young man, and very heedlessly," said my neighbor. "Look at Taillefer!—there, seated on that sofa at the corner of the fireplace. Mademoiselle Fanny is offering him a cup of coffee. He smiles. Would a murderer to whom that tale must have been torture, present so calm a face? Isn't his whole air patriarchal?"

"Yes; but go and ask him if he went to the war in Germany," I said.

"Why not?"

And with that audacity which is seldom lacking to women when some action attracts them, or their minds are impelled by curiosity, my neighbor went up to the purveyor.

"Were you ever in Germany?" she asked.

Taillefer came near dropping his cup and saucer.

"I, madame? No, never."

"What are you talking about, Taillefer"; said our host, interrupting him. "Were you not in the commissariat during the campaign of Wagram?"

"Ah, true!" replied Taillefer, "I was there at that time."

"You are mistaken," said my neighbor, returning to my side; "that's a good man."

"Well," I cried, "before the end of this evening, I will hunt that murderer out of the slough in which he is hiding."

Every day, before our eyes, a moral phenomenon of amazing profundity takes place which is, nevertheless, so simple as never to be noticed. If two men meet in a salon, one of whom has the right to hate or despise the other, whether from a knowledge of some private and latent fact which degrades him, or of a secret condition, or even of a coming revenge, those two men divine each other's souls, and are able to measure the gulf which separates or ought to separate them. They observe each other unconsciously; their minds are preoccupied by themselves; through their looks, their gestures, an indefinable emanation of their thought transpires; there's a magnet between them. I don't know which has the strongest power of attraction, vengeance or crime, hatred or insult. Like a priest who cannot consecrate the host in presence of an evil spirit, each is ill at ease and distrustful; one is polite, the other surly, but I know not which; one colors or turns pale, the other trembles. Often the avenger is as cowardly as the victim. Few men have the courage to invoke an evil, even when just or necessary, and men are silent or forgive a wrong from hatred of uproar or fear of some tragic ending.

This introsusception of our souls and our sentiments created a mysterious struggle between Taillefer and myself. Since the first inquiry I had put to him during Monsieur Hermann's narrative, he had steadily avoided my eye. Possibly he avoided those of all the other guests. He talked with the youthful, inexperienced daughter of the banker, feeling, no doubt, like many other criminals, a need of drawing near to innocence, hoping to find rest there. But, though I was a long distance from him, I heard him, and my piercing eye fascinated his. When he thought he could watch me unobserved our eyes met, and his eyelids dropped immediately.

Weary of this torture, Taillefer seemed determined to put an end to it by sitting down at a card-table. I at once went to bet on his adversary; hoping to lose my money. The wish was granted; the player left the table and I took his place, face to face with the murderer.

"Monsieur," I said, while he dealt the cards, "may I ask if you are Monsieur Frederic Taillefer, whose family I know very well at Beauvais?"

"Yes, monsieur," he answered.

He dropped the cards, turned pale, put his hands to his head and rose, asking one of the bettors to take his hand.

"It is too hot here," he cried; "I fear—"

He did not end the sentence. His face expressed intolerable suffering, and he went out hastily. The master of the house followed him and seemed to take an anxious interest in his condition. My neighbor and I looked at each other, but I saw a tinge of bitter sadness or reproach upon her countenance.

"Do you think your conduct is merciful?" she asked, drawing me to the embrasure of a window just as I was leaving the card-table, having lost all my money. "Would you accept the power of reading hearts? Why not leave things to human justice or divine justice? We may escape one but we cannot escape the other. Do you think the privilege of a judge of the court of assizes so much to be envied? You have almost done the work of an executioner."

"After sharing and stimulating my curiosity, why are you now lecturing me on morality?"

"You have made me reflect," she answered.

"So, then, peace to villains, war to the sorrowful, and let's deify gold! However, we will drop the subject," I added, laughing. "Do you see that young girl who is just entering the salon?"

"Yes, what of her?"

"I met her, three days ago, at the ball of the Neapolitan ambassador, and I am passionately in love with her. For pity's sake tell me her name. No one was able—"

"That is Mademoiselle Victorine Taillefer."

I grew dizzy.

"Her step-mother," continued my neighbor, "has lately taken her from a convent, where she was finishing, rather late in the day, her education. For a long time her father refused to recognize her. She comes here for the first time. She is very beautiful and very rich."

These words were accompanied by a sardonic smile.

At this moment we heard violent, but smothered outcries; they seemed to come from a neighboring apartment and to be echoed faintly back through the garden.

"Isn't that the voice of Monsieur Taillefer?" I said.

We gave our full attention to the noise; a frightful moaning reached our ears. The wife of the banker came hurriedly towards us and closed the window.

"Let us avoid a scene," she said. "If Mademoiselle Taillefer hears her father, she might be thrown into hysterics."

The banker now re-entered the salon, looked round for Victorine, and said a few words in her ear. Instantly the young girl uttered a cry, ran to the door, and disappeared. This event produced a great sensation. The card-players paused. Every one questioned his neighbor. The murmur of voices swelled, and groups gathered.

"Can Monsieur Taillefer be—" I began.

"—dead?" said my sarcastic neighbor. "You would wear the gayest mourning, I fancy!"

"But what has happened to him?"

"The poor dear man," said the mistress of the house, "is subject to attacks of a disease the name of which I never can remember, though Monsieur Brousson has often told it to me; and he has just been seized with one."

"What is the nature of the disease?" asked an examining-judge.

"Oh, it is something terrible, monsieur," she replied. "The doctors know no remedy. It causes the most dreadful suffering. One day, while the unfortunate man was staying at my country-house, he had an attack, and I was obliged to go away and stay with a neighbor to avoid hearing him; his cries were terrible; he tried to kill himself; his daughter was obliged to have him put into a strait-jacket and fastened to his bed. The poor man declares there are live animals in his head gnawing his brain; every nerve quivers with horrible shooting pains, and he writhes in torture. He suffers so much in his head that he did not even feel the moxas they used formerly to apply to relieve it; but Monsieur Brousson, who is now his physician, has forbidden that remedy, declaring that the trouble is a nervous affection, an inflammation of the nerves, for which leeches should be applied to the neck, and opium to the head. As a result, the attacks are not so frequent; they appear now only about once a year, and always late in the autumn. When he recovers, Taillefer says repeatedly that he would far rather die than endure such torture."

"Then he must suffer terribly!" said a broker, considered a wit, who was present.

"Oh," continued the mistress of the house, "last year he nearly died in one of these attacks. He had gone alone to his country-house on pressing business. For want, perhaps, of immediate help, he lay twenty-two hours stiff and stark as though he were dead. A very hot bath was all that saved him."

"It must be a species of lockjaw," said one of the guests.

"I don't know," she answered. "He got the disease in the army nearly thirty years ago. He says it was caused by a splinter of wood entering his head from a shot on board a boat. Brousson hopes to cure him.

They say the English have discovered a mode of treating the disease with prussic acid—"

At that instant a still more piercing cry echoed through the house, and froze us with horror.

"There! that is what I listened to all day long last year," said the banker's wife. "It made me jump in my chair and rasped my nerves dreadfully. But, strange to say, poor Taillefer, though he suffers untold agony, is in no danger of dying. He eats and drinks as well as ever during even short cessations of the pain—nature is so queer! A German doctor told him it was a form of gout in the head, and that agrees with Brousson's opinion."

I left the group around the mistress of the house and went away. On the staircase I met Mademoiselle Taillefer, whom a footman had come to fetch.

"Oh!" she said to me, weeping, "what has my poor father ever done to deserve such suffering?—so kind as he is!"

I accompanied her downstairs and assisted her in getting into the carriage, and there I saw her father bent almost double.

Mademoiselle Taillefer tried to stifle his moans by putting her handkerchief to his mouth; unhappily he saw me; his face became even more distorted, a convulsive cry rent the air, and he gave me a dreadful look as the carriage rolled away.

That dinner, that evening exercised a cruel influence on my life and on my feelings. I loved Mademoiselle Taillefer, precisely, perhaps, because honor and decency forbade me to marry the daughter of a murderer, however good a husband and father he might be. A curious fatality impelled me to visit those houses where I knew I could meet Victorine; often, after giving myself my word of honor to renounce the happiness of seeing her, I found myself that same evening beside her. My struggles were great. Legitimate love, full of chimerical remorse, assumed the color of a criminal passion. I despised myself for bowing to Taillefer when, by chance, he accompanied his daughter, but I bowed to him all the same.

Alas! for my misfortune Victorine is not only a pretty girl, she is also educated, intelligent, full of talent and of charm, without the slightest pedantry or the faintest tinge of assumption. She converses with reserve, and her nature has a melancholy grace which no one can resist. She loves me, or at least she lets me think so; she has a certain smile which she keeps for me alone; for me, her voice grows softer still. Oh, yes! she loves me! But she adores her father; she tells me of his kindness, his gentleness, his excellent qualities. Those praises are so many dagger-thrusts with which she stabs me to the heart.

One day I came near making myself the accomplice, as it were, of the crime which led to the opulence of the Taillefer family. I was on the point of asking the father for Victorine's hand. But I fled; I travelled; I went to Germany, to Andernach; and then—I returned! I found Victorine pale, and thinner; if I had seen her well in health and gay, I should certainly have been saved. Instead of which my love burst out again with untold violence. Fearing that my scruples might degenerate into monomania, I resolved to convoke a sanhedrim of sound consciences, and obtain from them some light on this problem of high morality and philosophy,—a problem which had been, as we shall see, still further complicated since my return.

Two days ago, therefore, I collected those of my friends to whom I attribute most delicacy, probity, and honor. I invited two Englishmen, the secretary of an embassy, and a puritan; a former minister, now a mature statesman; a priest, an old man; also my former guardian, a simple-hearted being who rendered so loyal a guardianship account that the memory of it is still green at the Palais; besides these, there were present a judge, a lawyer, and a notary,—in short, all social opinions, and all practical virtues.

We began by dining well, talking well, and making some noise; then, at dessert, I related my history candidly, and asked for advice, concealing, of course, the Taillefer name.

A profound silence suddenly fell upon the company. Then the notary took leave. He had, he said, a deed to draw.

The wine and the good dinner had reduced my former guardian to silence; in fact I was obliged later in the evening to put him under guardianship, to make sure of no mishap to him on his way home.

"I understand!" I cried. "By not giving an opinion you tell me energetically enough what I ought to do."

On this there came a stir throughout the assembly.

A capitalist who had subscribed for the children and tomb of General Foy exclaimed:—

"Like Virtue's self, a crime has its degrees."

"Rash tongue!" said the former minister, in a low voice, nudging me with his elbow.

"Where's your difficulty?" asked a duke whose fortune is derived from the estates of stubborn Protestants, confiscated on the revocation of the Edict of Nantes.

The lawyer rose, and said:—

"In law, the case submitted to us presents no difficulty. Monsieur le duc is right!" cried the legal organ. "There are time limitations. Where should we all be if we had to search into the origin of fortunes? This is simply an affair of conscience. If you must absolutely carry the case before some tribunal, go to that of the confessional."

The Code incarnate ceased speaking, sat down, and drank a glass of champagne. The man charged with the duty of explaining the gospel, the good priest, rose.

"God has made us all frail beings," he said firmly. "If you love the heiress of that crime, marry her; but content yourself with the property she derives from her mother; give that of the father to the poor."

"But," cried one of those pitiless hair-splitters who are often to be met with in the world, "perhaps the father could make a rich marriage only because he was rich himself; consequently, the marriage was the fruit of the crime."

"This discussion is, in itself, a verdict. There are some things on which a man does not deliberate," said my former guardian, who thought to enlighten the assembly with a flash of inebriety.

"Yes!" said the secretary of an embassy.

"Yes!" said the priest.

But the two men did not mean the same thing.

A "doctrinaire," who had missed his election to the Chamber by one hundred and fifty votes out of one hundred and fifty-five, here rose.

"Messieurs," he said, "this phenomenal incident of intellectual nature is one of those which stand out vividly from the normal condition to which sobriety is subjected. Consequently the decision to be made ought to be the spontaneous act of our consciences, a sudden conception, a prompt inward verdict, a fugitive shadow of our mental apprehension, much like the flashes of sentiment which constitute taste. Let us vote."

"Let us vote!" cried all my guests.

I have each two balls, one white, one red. The white, symbol of virginity, was to forbid the marriage; the red ball sanctioned it. I myself abstained from voting, out of delicacy.

My friends were seventeen in number; nine was therefore the majority. Each man put his ball into the wicker basket with a narrow throat, used to hold the numbered balls when card-players draw for their places at pool. We were all roused to a more or less keen curiosity; for this balloting to clarify morality was certainly original. Inspection of the ballot-box showed the presence of nine white balls! The result did not surprise me; but it came into my heard to count the young men of my own age whom I had brought to sit in judgment. These casuists were precisely nine in number; they all had the same thought.

"Oh, oh!" I said to myself, "here is secret unanimity to forbid the marriage, and secret unanimity to sanction it! How shall I solve that problem?"

"Where does the father-in-law live?" asked one my school-friends, heedlessly, being less sophisticated than the others.

"There's no longer a father-in-law," I replied. "Hitherto, my conscience has spoken plainly enough to make your verdict superfluous. If to-day its voice is weakened, here is the cause of my cowardice. I received, about two months ago, this all-seducing letter."

And I showed them the following invitation, which I took from my pocket-book:—

"You are invited to be present at the funeral procession, burial services, and interment of Monsieur Jean-Frederic Taillefer, of the house of Taillefer and Company, formerly Purveyor of Commissary-meats, in his lifetime chevalier of the Legion of honor, and of the Golden Spur, captain of the first company of the Grenadiers of the National Guard of Paris, deceased, May 1st, at his residence, rue Joubert; which will take place at, etc., etc. "On the part of, etc."

"Now, what am I do to?" I continued; "I will put the question before you in a broad way. There is undoubtedly a sea of blood in Mademoiselle Taillefer's estates; her inheritance from her father is a vast

Aceldama. I know that. *But* Prosper Magnan left no heirs; *but*, again, I have been unable to discover the family of the merchant who was murdered at Andernach. To whom therefore can I restore that fortune? And ought it to be wholly restored? Have I the right to betray a secret surprised by me,—to add a murdered head to the dowry of an innocent girl, to give her for the rest of her life bad dreams, to deprive her of all her illusions, and say, 'Your gold is stained with blood'? I have borrowed the 'Dictionary of Cases of Conscience' from an old ecclesiastic, but I can find nothing there to solve my doubts. Shall I found pious masses for the repose of the souls of Prosper Magnan, Wahlenfer, and Taillefer? Here we are in the middle of the nineteenth century! Shall I build a hospital, or institute a prize for virtue? A prize for virtue would be given to scoundrels; and as for hospitals, they seem to me to have become in these days the protectors of vice. Besides, such charitable actions, more or less profitable to vanity, do they constitute reparation?— and to whom do I owe reparation? But I love; I love passionately. My love is my life. If I, without apparent motive, suggest to a young girl accustomed to luxury, to elegance, to a life fruitful of all enjoyments of art, a young girl who loves to idly listen at the opera to Rossini's music,—if to her I should propose that she deprive herself of fifteen hundred thousand francs in favor of broken-down old men, or scrofulous paupers, she would turn her back on me and laugh, or her confidential friend would tell her that I'm a crazy jester. If in an ecstasy of love, I should paint to her the charms of a modest life, and a little home on the banks of the Loire; if I were to ask her to sacrifice her Parisian life on the altar of our love, it would be, in the first place, a virtuous lie; in the next, I might only be opening the way to some painful experience; I might lose the heart of a girl who loves society, and balls, and personal adornment, and *me* for the time being. Some slim and jaunty officer, with a well-frizzed moustache, who can play the piano, quote Lord Byron, and ride a horse elegantly, may get her away from me. What shall I do? For Heaven's sake, give me some advice!"

The honest man, that species of puritan not unlike the father of Jeannie Deans, of whom I have already told you, and who, up to the present moment hadn't uttered a word, shrugged his shoulders, as he looked at me and said:—

"Idiot! why did you ask him if he came from Beauvais?"

ADDENDUM

The following personages appear in other stories of the Human Comedy.

        Taillefer, Jean-Frederic
          The Firm of Nucingen
          Father Goriot
          The Magic Skin

        Taillefer, Victorine
          Father Goriot

Made in the USA
Middletown, DE
08 September 2018